World's
Greatest
Cupcake
Recipe

International
Badminton
Championship

MISS FORSYTHIA MAYWEATHER

ROYAL
READING ALOUD
COMPETITION
FIRST
PLACE

FIRST
PLACE

WORLD'S BEST
Elephant Acrobatics
Trainer

Vincent X. Kirsch

Forsythia & Me

Farrar Straus Giroux · *New York*

To Jill Davis, who has made every day like Christmas

Distributed in Canada by D&M Publishers, Inc.

Color separations by Chroma Graphics

Printed in September 2010 in China by Toppan Leefung Printing Ltd.,

Dongguan City, Guangdong Province

First edition, 2011

1 3 5 7 9 10 8 6 4 2

www.fsgkidsbooks.com

Library of Congress Cataloging-in-Publication Data

Kirsch, Vincent X.

 Forsythia & me / Vincent X. Kirsch.— 1st ed.

  p. cm.

 Summary: Chester has always been in awe of his best friend's accomplishments, but when she becomes ill, he discovers
that he is capable of doing amazing things to entertain her while she is bed-ridden.

 ISBN: 978-0-374-32438-4

 [1. Best friends—Fiction.   2. Friendship—Fiction.   3. Helpfulness—Fiction.   4. Sharing—Fiction.   5. Humorous
stories.]   I. Title.   II. Title: Forsythia and me.

PZ7.K6383Fo 2011

[E]—dc22

                                                                                    2009053233

*F*orsythia and I are best friends. She does things that amaze me.

Forsythia can decorate the most incredible birthday cakes I have ever seen. This year she flew out of the cake she had made just for me.

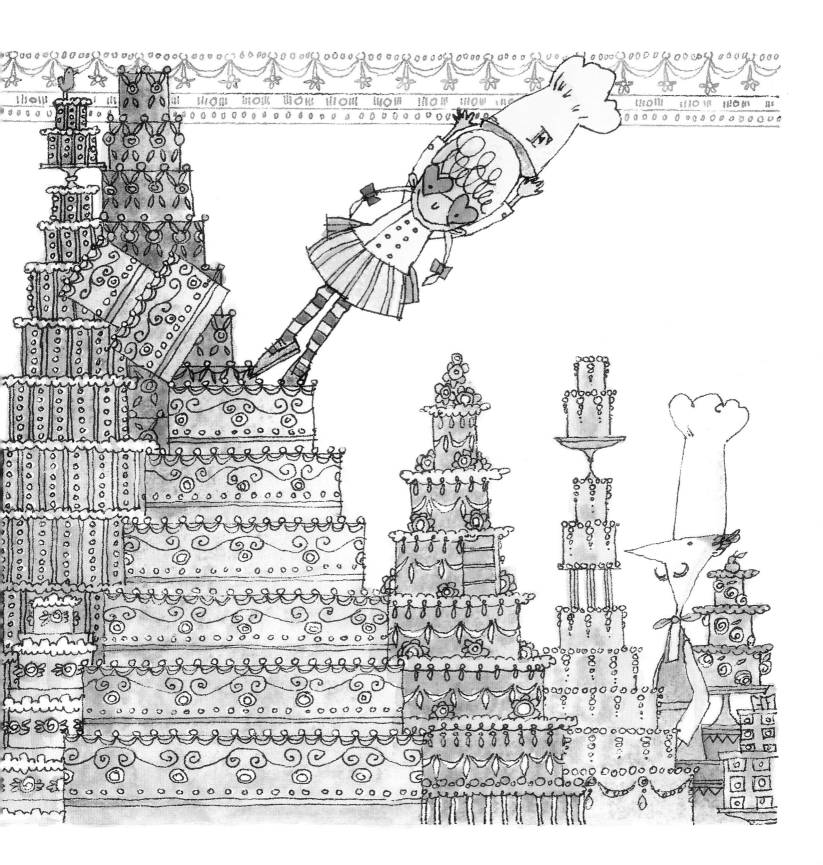

She can play Sergei Ratzinsinski's Piano Concerto No. 7 in B major. She can play it backwards and upside down if I ask her to.

Forsythia grows prizewinning roses that are a very unusual shade of purple. She even gets them to bloom in the middle of winter.

On Saturday afternoons, Forsythia performs in the circus. She has to lend me a pair of binoculars so that I can find her.

On Sunday afternoons, Forsythia dances in the ballet. I am glad to say I have no trouble whatsoever finding her there.

Forsythia fearlessly tames the ferocious animals at the city zoo. She has trained them so well that they never arrive late for tea.

When Forsythia was asked to paint the portraits of the royal family and their royal pets, she was able to paint them from memory with a blindfold on. I noticed that the royal jester looked a lot like me.

One day, Forsythia was not feeling very well and had to cancel her sold-out spectacular figure-skating show. She tried everything to feel better, but nothing worked.

I had an idea. I baked a cupcake for her and decorated it with her initial.

"Thank you, Chester. That is exactly what I needed!" she said from under the blankets.

I played "Chopsticks" for her and made only thirteen mistakes.

"That was beautiful. Would you please play it again?" Forsythia asked between sneezes.

I picked a bouquet for her. The flowers just happened to be called forsythia. "Can you believe there is a flower named after me?" she exclaimed.

I did an acrobatic trick that I had been practicing for weeks.

"Chester, I have never seen anyone do that before!" Forsythia remarked.

Forsythia hummed her favorite ballet music as I danced a pirate's jig that I made up right on the spot.

"Would you please teach that to me?" she begged.

1

Hop on your left foot three times while bending your other knee.

4

Kick your right leg up in front.

7

Run away in the opposite direction.

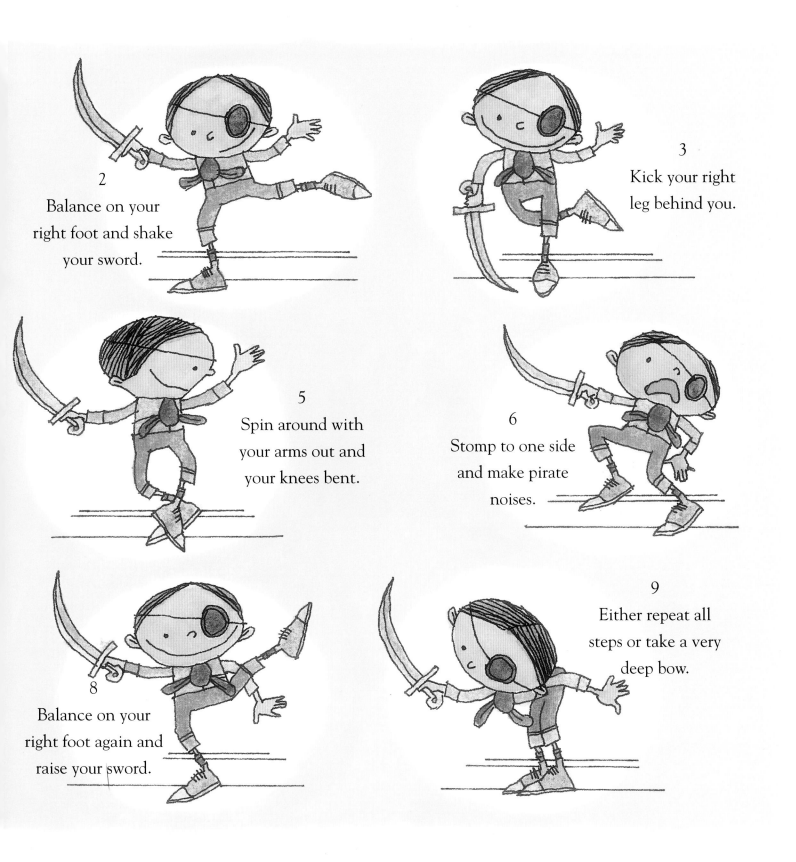

2
Balance on your right foot and shake your sword.

3
Kick your right leg behind you.

5
Spin around with your arms out and your knees bent.

6
Stomp to one side and make pirate noises.

8
Balance on your right foot again and raise your sword.

9
Either repeat all steps or take a very deep bow.

I arranged all of Forsythia's stuffed animals since she didn't want to stay in bed anymore.

"That looks perfect! I am feeling so much better, and it's time for tea!" she told me.

I drew a picture of Forsythia and did it with one of my eyes covered. She blushed and said, "Chester, you amaze me! You even made me look like a princess!"

Soon enough, we went outside to play. Forsythia was quite happy to perform her spectacular figure-skating show . . . just for me!